About the Author

RUSSELL LYNES (1910–1991) was an art historian, cultural critic, author, photographer, and managing editor of *Harper's Magazine*. His articles for *Harper's* and *Life* in 1949 made parsing American culture into highbrow, middlebrow, and lowbrow a national pastime. He wrote many books, including *Snobs* and *The Tastemakers*.

GUESTS

GUESTS

or,
How to Survive Hospitality:
The Classic Guidebook

RUSSELL LYNES

With Casual Drawings by the Author

HARPER

NEW YORK • LONDON • TORONTO • SYDNEY

HARPER

HarperCollins books may be purchased for educational, business, or sales
promotional use. For information please write: Special Markets Department,
HarperCollins Publishers, 10 East 53rd Street, New York, NY 10022.

FIRST HARPER PAPERBACK PUBLISHED 2009.

Library of Congress Cataloging-in-Publication Data is available upon
request.

ISBN 978-0-06-170641-7 (Harper paperback)

09 10 11 12 13 /CW 10 9 8 7 6 5 4 3 2 1

TO
E.R.L. AND G.P.L. II
who, I am told, are excellent
guests

Any resemblance that the reader may find between the characters in this book and any actual persons, living or dead, should be a lesson to him about the company he keeps.

Contents

GUESTS

I. Oh, the Times! Oh, the Customs!

GUESTS in the house have always seemed to me to present an opportunity for imminent catastrophe. In all social intercourse there is the element of risk. The ill-chosen moment for the carefully chosen compliment, the innocent misunderstanding, the simple *gaffe*, the unpredictable temper—these are always lurking in the background, threatening to strike the most casual of social relationships as well as the most complicated ones.

But to invite people to one's home, or to allow oneself to be the subject of an invitation is to expose oneself to any number of unforeseen difficulties. Everyone knows this, and yet nearly everyone is content to blunder along, exposing himself and his friends and acquaintances to difficulties that he might readily avoid. It speaks well for our resilience and the shortness of our memories that we have not all become hermits long since.

The reason why we have not withdrawn into cells is not only our natural gregariousness but the development of certain rituals of social behavior which make it possible to visit and be visited, safeguards which have grown up through usage to protect us from our friends and our friends from us. Added to the rituals, which in a more formal era than our own were enough to make people go home at a reasonable hour, to appear for meals on time, and to observe certain other amenities now in disuse, are the techniques which have been devised (or perhaps I should say improvised) to deal with all sorts of social situations in which guests are a problem.

I should like to set forth in this little book some of the problems most commonly faced both by guests and hosts in the delicate relationships that exist between them, to examine some types of situations in which mere people become guests, and guests become threats to civilized living.

But before launching into specifics, I should explain that my interest in this problem goes back to my early childhood and was almost surely set off by an incident provoked by my older brother when he was about four. My father at that time was the rector of a church in a small but prospering New England town that boasted two small manufacturing plants, two churches besides his own, and a bandstand in front of the Town Hall where Saturday night concerts brought the entire town to lie on the grass and watch the fireflies and hear what seemed to me beautiful music. The rectory, which was next to the Town Hall, was built in the Queen Anne manner, with a brown shingled peaked tower at one corner, a veranda with spindle work hidden by wisteria, and stained glass in the stair-landing windows. The rectory, as rectories are wont to be, was in the center of the town's focus, and what went on there was everybody's business.

Father was in his early thirties and, having got a late start in the ministry, was new in his first parish. He was zealous, but being a New Englander himself, he was aware that whatever overtures he made to his new parishioners must be cordial but cautious and unassuming. He knew that the most he could expect from his flock for the first few years of his incumbency was not warmth but a gradually decreasing chill, and he proceeded accordingly to try with his easy humor to thaw a vestryman here and a Women's Auxiliary member there as occasion arose. He was doing rather well, and my mother, whose blond good looks must have stirred envy or worse in many a local breast, went at the business of being a minister's wife with all the zest for it that she could summon. My father had been a lawyer when she married him, and when he turned late to the cloth, the adjustment was harder on his wife than on him. But she gave herself to it with good grace and with rather more dedication to her man than to his profession.

My brother, who should never have been a minister's son, started early to speak his mind. The Women's Auxiliary, which sewed things for something known vaguely as "missions," met on Wednesdays, and my mother decided that the parish house was a dreary place for them to forgather and so she invited them to the rectory. They sat around in as much of a circle as the parlor with its mixture of Victorian and mission furniture permitted, and sewed. They may have gossiped too, but I was too young at the time to have much sense of what went on. In fact the only meeting of the Auxiliary that made any impression on me was the one at which my brother became notorious.

I have this second hand, but the story as it has been retold to me is a simple one. My brother, returning from a walk with his nurse, marched into the middle of the parlor and stood for a minute surveying the ladies, who looked up from their sewing. He sized up each one of the ten or twelve who sat around him, and then he singled out one and walked straight to her.

"I certainly don't like you," he said, and then turned away, walked across the room without hesitation to another of the women, and said to her, "But I do like you."

It is not hard to imagine what this did to the immediate circle or how fast the news spread through the town. Those who took the part of the lady my brother disliked said that he never would have said such a thing unless

"I certainly don't like you. . . ."

5

he had heard it from his parents (they underestimated my brother, even at the age of four), and those who were friends of the lady he had singled out for his affection thought the same thing but were delighted that the new minister and his wife had such good sense. The spurned woman "cried and took on," as they say in that part of New England, and was not to be comforted. Mother sent her flowers with a note which must have been solemnly composed through a night of anguish; father went to call.

It was a traumatic experience all around, except for my brother, who rather enjoyed the stir his honest expression had precipitated, and it left its mark on me. Visiting in people's houses or having people visit in our house was for a long time something to be regarded with caution if not dismay, to be approached only with the eyes wide open and the mouth tight shut.

A single cloud of gloom that hung over the rectory for years and years did nothing to dispel my suspicion of guests. The cloud was known as "parish calls," and they were something father had to "make." He was not one to press himself on people, and he regarded parish calls as an invasion of privacy in which, if they had not been ordained by God and expected by the vestry, he never would have indulged.

Some of the parishioners returned his calls and so appeared at the rectory. If father retired with one of them to his study, my brother and I knew it meant business and we stayed away, but if he settled down with them in the parlor we were aware that this was merely a polite call which father would be glad to terminate as soon as might be. In the rectory, where my family indulged in the shocking policy of allowing games even on Sunday, my brother and I were always on the lookout for visits we could break up, and as though by tacit agreement with father we would find seemingly innocent ways of intervening. Our most common, as well as one of our most successful, methods was to take up positions at either end of the hall outside the parlor and quietly roll a ball back and forth. On about the fourth toss it would roll into the parlor under the sofa on which visitors always sat. One of us would appear in the door and find that father was unceremoniously down on his hands and knees groping for the ball. In due course he would emerge with it in his hand and say sternly, "Now that's enough of that. You children run along." Almost invariably the visitor would respond with, "Well, I must be running along myself," and off he would go. Even as children we developed a certain delight in the oblique powers of suggestion, a social lesson that everyone should assimilate at an early age.

The powers of suggestion, however, worked in other ways. One incident which took place at the rectory made a deep impression on me and in a way epitomized the hazards both of being a caller and being called upon. My mother had arranged by telephone for a woman she did not know to come and clean, and when someone showed up in the course of the morning, mother took her to the kitchen and showed her where the mops and brooms were kept and told her what she wanted done first. The woman was not the cleaning woman, but a parishioner come to return father's call.

It is a long while since I have lived in a rectory, and it may be that life in a minister's home has suffered little change, but in the past quarter of a century there have been substantial changes in social mores elsewhere which have altered the relationship between guest and host. There was a time not long ago, for example, when a lady would get into her carriage or car and spend the afternoon "dropping cards" on her acquaintances, hoping in her heart that everyone she might call on would be out dropping cards on her. To an earlier generation this custom was known as the "morning call" though it was not likely to take place in the morning. In the words of a nineteenth-century expert on manners, "morning in fashionable parlance means any time before dinner." This same expert warned that: "The conversation at a morning call must be light enough not to disturb digestion or take away the appetite." The proper call lasted not less than ten minutes and not more than fifteen, and if you happened to be called upon by more than one visitor at a time, you were cautioned that: "Morning visitors are not to be introduced to each other, unless you are sure that it will be mutually agreeable."

Just what sort of tension this established between two morning callers who sat and glared at each other, unintroduced because their hostess did not think that they were "mutually agreeable," is difficult for our generation to picture. But in any case neither one stayed more than a few minutes, and both tried not to upset their hostess's digestion or spoil her appetite.

When being polite was taken care of by such rituals and the amenities were observed by impersonal formalities, anyone could learn how to cope with almost any social situation by reference to a book of etiquette. But there have been two marked changes in social behavior which have altered all this. One is the recent emphasis on "casual" entertaining and informal living, and the other is much more subtle and, I believe, more fundamental. It is our insistence that we have a God-given right not to be bored.

Look back again a full generation, and you will see what I mean. Consider the furniture in the parlor and the ways in which people sat on the straight-backed chairs, their spines erect, their knees pressed together. Recall, if you can, the polite conversation in which any display of emotion was considered gauche and any topic which might incite argument was rigorously avoided. Even laughter, if it was hearty, was regarded, especially for women, as not quite nice.*

In those days one accepted as part of one's social duties the necessity to be bored at least part of the time; now we consider it an outrage if we have to put up with a single boring evening. But since we are unsure of ourselves as hosts and equally unsure of our acquaintances as avenues of escape from boredom, we are likely to shift the responsibility for entertaining either to a mechanical gadget like the television set or the home movie, or to the risks of abundant liquor, or to games such as bridge, canasta, "the game," or any other device which makes guests as painless as possible.†

It is our preoccupation with informality and casualness that lays us wide open to most of the hazards from guests. As hosts there are no longer prescribed tunes for us to call. In sacrificing the rituals and formalities of a more decorous age we have exposed our flanks; our homes

* "When you laugh, don't talk; and when there is talking to be done, be sure and not laugh. Smile if you please, and there is occasion for it. You need not look absolutely stupid." *The Illustrated Manners Book,* New York, 1855.

† The wire (or tape) recorder has lately been introduced as an implement of social diversion. It is often used surreptitiously, so that the guests are unaware that their conversation is being recorded. In recent months I have several times been subjected to hearing playbacks of former parties. There is nothing quite so flaccid as a recording of the late, hilarious stages of a party one did not attend.

are no longer our castles. We can no longer pull up the drawbridge of our reticence and drop the portcullis of our offended sensibilities. Our latchstrings, for better or for worse, are always half out.

The price of our era's informal hospitality is lack of privacy. Our refusal to be bored leads us into the paths of informality, and informality leaves us the defenseless quarry of all comers, but it is a price we have decided to pay. Since none of us is going to gainsay hospitality as a virtue, or cease to practice it, we may as well face it realistically. I started at an early age. Nearly all of the problems of hospitality arose in the rectory, and all of them seemed to be raised to a higher power; a clergyman is somehow expected to enjoy being imposed upon. If he turns away a guest, it is considered not merely an unfriendly but an un-Christian act. Our house was always full of people whose own houses had just burned down, or whose bank accounts were exhausted, or whose families would no longer put up with them. Our guest of longest duration was an ex-railroad man in his eighties who just settled in the guest room and stayed for nearly three years. He died there one night in his sleep.

II. Bores

IT WAS not until long after my first encounter with guests as a child that I realized that some guests were boring and some were not. The comings and goings in the rectory were constant, and some of the people who came I liked and others I didn't. Sometimes I was told to "run along," as I have said; sometimes when callers came I was allowed to stay and "sit quietly" or even go on with my games on the floor. What it was that set up hostility in me toward some adults and made me a little social menace or a sullen lump and what warmed me toward others was something I did not understand for a long while. Now I can say that some of those adults were bores and some were not.

Let me explain what I mean. We select our friends because they are not bores; or, to put it another way, because they do not think that we are bores. Some of

the adults who invaded the rectory were not in the least
interested in me, no matter how polite their protestations
to the contrary, and I felt it, even if I didn't know it.
Others, however, seemed to share my world in spite of
their size. My world did not bore them; so I liked them.

Host

More often than not a bore is merely a convenient
label we give to a person whom we do not fascinate, and
just as often these bores are socially essential to us. If
it weren't for them, we should have nothing against
which to measure our sophistication, and we should be
compelled to admit that we are bores ourselves.

It is probably this that explains why everyone entertains boring guests at some time or other, and why one constantly encounters them in other people's houses. We don't invite them just out of social duty (though we may tell ourselves that we do); we invite them because they do something for our self-esteem.

It also explains the large (and often unmanageable) party as an institution. At a cocktail party, for instance, the host is the only individual who never gets trapped. It is his duty, recognized by everyone, to move about the room, to bestow his favors everywhere but never long in any one place. Cocktail shaker in hand he fills a glass here, makes a polite inquiry there, says a few words of greeting, gets a forlorn guest attached to a conversational group, and moves on, his social duty being for once to spread himself as thin as possible. If he sees a woman carefully examining the *bibelots* on the table, or thumbing a magazine, or looking at a drawing on the wall with complete absorption, he will know that she is teeming inside with feelings of neglect. No matter what her social gifts, no matter whether she is a bore or not, he can easily manipulate her into conversation with her opposite number, a male who for some unaccountable reason has taken an intense interest in reading the titles on the backs of the record albums. Whether they bore each other once the host has got them face to face is their business. The host moves on to other matters with a sense of accomplishment, with a feeling of satisfied generalship which reminds him of Horace's comment: "A host is like a general: it takes a mishap to reveal his genius."

Unfortunately, however, the cocktail party, which is more blessed to give than to receive, often has to be attended in somebody else's house, and it is there that the whole business takes on quite a different complexion. There you may easily find yourself (having momentarily forgotten the only essential rule of cocktail party behavior: never sit down on a sofa) trapped by a bore from whom nothing short of overt rudeness can save you.

I have studied the bore at a great many parties, dinner parties, literary teas, wedding receptions, and other sociable gatherings, including conventions, testimonial luncheons, and church "socials," and I have found that some can be distinguished by facial types, some by the cut of their clothes, and some by their eagerly roving eyes which are so obviously searching for a quarry. These methods of distinguishing which people to avoid are, however, too subjective to pass along, and are only partially reliable even after long practice. The sad thing about most bores is that they cannot be distinguished at a distance: it is only when one is face to face with them (or side by side with them) in a situation from which it is next to impossible to withdraw that one is aware, too late, of their special alchemy for turning golden moments into lead.

The common varieties of bores are well known to everyone. Ambrose Bierce said that a bore is "a person who talks when you want him to listen," but as apt as the definition is, the species is a good deal more complicated than that. There are, for example, many gradations of boredom, such as the Crashing Bore whose conversation weighs on you like an actual physical burden that you want to throw off because it is stifling you, and quite a different kind, the Tinkling Bore whose conversation bothers you in the way that an insistent fly does, annoying but not dangerous. There are such types as the Still Waters Run Deep variety who defy you to say anything that will change the expression on their faces much less elicit an encouraging word from them. There you are on the sofa with them, their intense eyes peering at you with something between hopelessness and scorn, impressing on you the deep reservoir of their self-sufficiency and challenging you to ruffle the waters that lurk there. I cite this merely as an example of the passive as opposed to the militant type (both the Crashing and the Tinkling are militant), for it is those who make you feel like a bore who are the most boring of all.

But let us get to more specific types that one is likely to encounter at a strawberry festival, cocktail party, wedding reception, or other carnival. You have arrived early . . . not before the time for which you were invited, of course, but less than an hour after the appointed hour, so that the party is not yet in full swing. There are just a few people; not yet as many people as there are chairs, so you have no choice but to sit down next to or at least near someone. There is a better than even chance that you may be rooted for the next half hour, though as the place fills up you will be able to plant a lady in your chair and slip away on the pretext of getting yourself another drink.

For the moment, however, you are planted; your party smile pulls your lips back in a pose of amiability, and you are prepared for whatever line the conversation may take. You may even be ready to establish a line yourself, once the feeling-out process has been got through, but the chances are that the lady, for you are next to a lady, will, according to custom, take the initiative. She may, indeed, try to "draw you out," in which case she has indicated that she is quite willing to be on the receiving end, and if anyone is going to be bored, she is prepared to accept the burden.

The risk, of course, is that you may fall for her pretty bait and embark on a line of conversation that is more involved or more serious than is generally considered suitable to a party, and slowly you become aware that your voice is beginning to drone. While the lady's polite smile continues to egg you on, her eyes look beyond you to the group that is standing in front of the fireplace at the far side of the room. You are aware, all at **once, that** you are being a bore, and that you have

The Good Listener

been put in this position by a species known as a Good Listener.

It is customary to think of the Good Listener as a "social asset," and many children are taught by their parents, at an early age, as I was, how to be a Good

Listener. But a Good Listener's ultimate social contribution is to make bores out of other people. His bright eyes and inviting smile mask a profound indifference to what anyone else says, and his basic rule of behavior is that it pays better to cock an ear than to cock a snook. In that sense he is a bore himself, just as much of a bore as that other social "asset," the Fascinating Conversationalist.

It is difficult to assemble a gaggle of people without including at least one Fascinating Conversationalist. He naturally gravitates to large parties because he is strictly an audience man and anecdotalist, and he is easy to distinguish in any gathering. He talks in a voice filled with the authority of complete self-possession and with a volume a trifle louder than most of the other guests, as he likes to project himself beyond his immediate circle of listeners and, if possible, to increase it to encompass the entire company. His dress is inclined to exhibit some minor eccentricity which sets him slightly but not outlandishly apart from other people, such as a flower in the lapel, or tremendous moonstone cuff links, or a long cigarette holder, or possibly even a monocle hung around his neck on a black thread. His conversation is entirely anecdotal with innuendoes of a slightly scandalous nature, carefully gauged to exhibit his urbanity and wide acquaintance among well-known personages. He refers to celebrities by their first names, or even better, by their nicknames. Once he has started on a story about his good friend "Willie" Maugham, he will embroider it until it is as encrusted with ornament as a bishop's chasuble and about as suitable to a cocktail party.

The Fascinating Conversationalist

The fact that he is often the hostess's delight should not dim one to the fact that he is the bane of other guests. He is not a conversationalist at all but a monologist, and I contend he is one of the more virulent species of party bore.

The cocktail party is not, of course, the only social

device for gathering bores together, but it is one of the
most common. It is more than likely to be a one-fell-
swoop party at which one repays an overdue accumula-
tion of social obligations. And so it is apt to be made
up of the people one "ought to do something about,"
which is another name for the people one doesn't want
to have for dinner but should. A dinner has to be planned
with some attention to whether the guests are going to
like each other or not, or as some unscrupulous hosts
plan them, with an eye to whether the guests are such an
unlikely mixture that there are bound to be fireworks.
The cocktail party, as good a symbol of the informality
of modern entertaining as any, is, in a sense, a display
of social irresponsibility.* A host and hostess usually
invite a nucleus of close friends who can be depended
on to keep the liquor flowing and the *canapés* in circula-
tion and perhaps even to rescue the most flagrantly
miserable strays who are unable to fend for themselves.
Beyond that, it is every man and woman for him- or
herself.

It is not that the people one invites to a cocktail party
are bores; it is the necessity that each one feels to get the
most out of the ordeal somehow that makes them such.
Not long ago I found myself mustered into service at a
party given by close friends, and I was busily making

* To T. S. Eliot, who wrote a play about it, it is something
much more serious than that, though I am not quite sure what.

martinis in a large pitcher at a table in the corner of the dining room. A few people, besides myself, had taken refuge there from the crush in the living room, and one of them, a man I hadn't met before began to tell me a

Guest of Honor

long story about a nursery that was supposed to deliver
some lilac bushes to his place in Salisbury, Connecticut,
and had planted them by mistake in his neighbor's front
yard so that the neighbor, who was very proud of his
lawn and didn't like having holes dug in it, had ripped
up the bushes in a rage and had planted them across
his (the first man's) driveway so that he couldn't get
his car in. He would get out a sentence and a half and
be frustrated by someone asking me for a drink. Each
time he would take up where he left off. Not a detail
was sacrificed. I was forced to examine every sap-filled
twig of those bushes and every damp handful of dirt
from the holes, until finally, many interruptions later,
we arrived at the point which was intended to illustrate
something I had said casually about bad temper but by
that time could no longer remember.

I was, however, reminded of a doctrine of social behavior impressed on me by my mother. If you are interrupted in the course of telling a story, never try to finish
it unless you are asked to. It is a difficult rule to practice,
and if I don't observe it, I am at least aware of its virtues.

This sort of Total Recall Bore is one of the commonest
types, but it takes one of Spartan endurance to perform ad-
equately in the late stages of a cocktail party. By that time
other types have taken over—the Hilarious Laugher,
the Lapel Hanger, and other Life of the Party types*

---

* Especially those types who, when you say, "Oh, don't go,"
stay.

familiar enough to anyone who stays beyond the moment
when those who have plans for dinner have gone about
their business, and those who haven't, haven't.

The cocktail party emerged as a social institution at
just about the moment when the lavish dinner party
with its ten or twelve courses and five or six wines went
into eclipse. It was also the moment at which the books
of etiquette were giving up the battle for chaperones for
all unmarried women up to the age of twenty-five and
when social arbiters ceased to be shocked by young ladies
applying powder and lipstick in public. Naturally
enough, the older generation felt with grave concern
that such marked relaxation of the standards of behavior
signaled a general decline in public morality. But if their
rigid rules of deportment now seem to us to have been
oppressive, we must admit that they at least had some
formulas for taking care of the bores. As we look back
upon such devices as the dance card and the "fifteen-
minute formal call," it is apparent that the avoidance of
being stuck for long with a bore was a primary concern
of social planning. We have no such devices today.

When the buffet supper supplanted the formal dinner,
the problem of who talks with whom was transferred
from the hostess to the guests. A clever hostess could
frequently arrange the seating at her table so that everyone was assured of being next to someone he or she

might enjoy. Now both food and partners have become a matter of potluck. At a dinner party the chances are that the person with whom you have been conversing over cocktails will not be next to you when you get to the table. At a buffet it is your duty to get food for the lady you have been talking with, and it is conceivable that you might put in three hours struggling for conversation with someone with whom you have nothing in common but the fact that you are both balancing plates on your knees.

Some types of bores have no opportunity to show their true colors at a cocktail party; it takes a long evening to give them a chance to perform, and in this respect the dinner, whether buffet or not, is their most congenial medium. There are too many long-evening bores to mention them all, but there are a few typical ones which everyone encounters.

The first of these is the Noncommittal type who when asked his opinion about anything invariably exposes the fact that he hasn't any by insisting that "I always reserve judgment until I know all the facts." Conversation with this type is nearly impossible, which is just as well, and it is a good deal less risky than with his opposite, the Know All the Answers type. He can never let the conversation get beyond the first few sentences without at least figuratively taking you by the lapel and saying, "Now listen to me." He rarely leads the conversation, but wherever it goes, whether it has to do with Asiatic politics or modern painting, or national parks, or the life cycle of the salmon, he is right with it. "Listen, fellow," he will say, "you don't know what you're talking about." When you skewer him with an irrefutable argument

"I'm so stupid, I wouldn't know about that!"

or a precisely applied statistic, he wriggles free with, "That's not what my sources tell me." If the going really gets rough for him, he takes to imputing motives. "Why, man, that's Red talk," he'll fling at you, or if that is too farfetched, he'll raise his eyebrows quizzically and ask, "What's your angle? You got money in this?"

The opposite of this type is likely to be a woman of the Poor Stupid Little Me sort who hasn't an opinion about anything. She can mangle any conversational gambit by declaring, "Oh, I wouldn't know anything about *that.*" There is a male variation of this type who acts from quite different motives but produces much the same effect. He is the kind who says "I wouldn't know about that" in such a deprecating way as to imply that he is much too busy with the really important matters of life to bother with such frivolities as those which concern you. "I haven't time to read a book or get to a show. Too busy. Haven't read a book in years."

These sorts are all on the defensive, unlike such types as the Travel Bores, who are always just back from somewhere you wish they had stayed, or the Statistical Bores, who regale you with facts and figures about such subjects as the mean temperature of July and the recent variations from it, or the familiar Post-Mortem kind who replay their golf game for you divot by divot. Potentially none of these types are bores. It is only that you make them so by not having traveled where they have, not caring about weather statistics or not playing golf. Their enthusiasm, even though you cannot share it, has a somewhat infectious quality, and you are at least eager to interrupt them so that you can steer their enthusiasm to something that might interest you more.

This is not true of the Bored Bore, whose attempt at

sophistication takes the form of letting you know that everything bores him. If you have any enthusiasms of your own which you have been unguarded enough to mention, the Bored Bore will do his best to make you feel naïve about them. He has a sour word to say for the book you had thought was clever, the play you thought entertaining, or the woman you have found enchanting. His own boredom is all-encompassing. He listens to you as though he has heard everything you have to say before and better said; he refuses your offer of a drink with the disdain of a reformed alcoholic, and he looks at your wife as though he has known hundreds of her sort and thought them all tiresome. His kind is often emulated by teen-agers who believe his pose to be one of true sophistication.

It is not unusual to be saddled with this type by a hostess who uses the most enervating of all introductions: "I want you two to meet each other. You have so much in common." This is a cliché that inevitably sows the seeds of mutual suspicion, ruffles the poise of both and tends to dry up the conversational wells. It is second only in obtuseness to another substandard and wholly unsportsmanlike gambit: "I want you to meet Mrs. Green. Mrs. Green always says such witty things." Mrs. Green hates you on sight because she can't think of anything witty to say, and you hate yourself for not being able to give Mrs. Green a lead that will restore her composure.

For putting you in such an awkward spot, you both think that your hostess is not only a bore but a social cripple as well.

This business of pairing guests is sometimes carried to an extreme in which whole parties are built around the concept that if you get two "very interesting" people together they are going to make a fascinating evening for everybody. This is assumed to be particularly true of authors, yet nothing could be further from the truth. Authors are very likely to elbow their way to the center of the floor (since they are always hoping to be lionized) and they are not in the least prone to share it with anyone else. There is nothing essentially wrong with two authors at a party if they can be kept apart, each with his own circle of listeners. But if you get them face to face, you will find that they will spend the evening telling each other about the reviews of their latest books, how many copies they have sold, and the amount of advertising space their respective publishers have bought for them. If their conversation doesn't take this turn, and they both assume a modest pose (not uncommon among really successful writers), they spend their time patting each other gently on the back in one of the coldest kinds of love feasts one is ever likely to witness. There is a third turn that such an encounter may take. Some time ago in Paris several young literary lion-hunters managed to arrange a meeting between James

Two Authors in Conversation

Joyce and Marcel Proust, who had never encountered each other before. The young hunters waited breathlessly to see what these literary giants would say, pencils figuratively poised to record the meeting of these two great minds. Both men were ill; Joyce nearly blind, Proust suffering from acute asthma. They spent the evening talking about their symptoms; literature was never mentioned. A biographer and a novelist may often put on an entertaining show since they are not competitors; two novelists, two poets, two biographers almost never.

Sometimes the pairing of bores, however, has definite advantages. If you can get the Oversympathetic Bore with the Pathos Bore, you have made them both happy. The former is the sort who is so terribly kind and understanding that she (for it is usually a woman) quite literally looks for trouble so that she can be soothing. If you have been ill, the oversympathetic type can quickly make you bored with your own illness—something of a feat. The Pathos Bore, on the other hand, is the type to whom everything dreadful happens and who has always either come straight from the bedside of a sick friend or has been up all night with someone who has lost a "dear one," or has just dragged herself (she only moves by dragging herself) out of bed where she has been suffering "the tortures of the damned" from a headache, backache, or other psychosomatic or traumatic experience. If the Oversympathetic and Pathos types can be maneuvered into a corner with a third type, a threatened evening can sometimes be saved from destruction. This third bore, the Stiff Upper Lip kind makes the obvious final addition to the triumvirate. This is the sort who makes the gay gesture calculated to expose (not conceal) his unhappy lot. "Oh, it was nothing," he'll say. "The tooth wasn't badly impacted. They only had to take out one good one besides the bad one to stop the pain."

My wife's grandmother insisted that there were five forbidden subjects of conversation, forbidden, that is, on the grounds that they were boring. They were known to her and propounded to her family as the "Five D's" and they reflect not only the language but the social amenities of her time. They were: Domiciles, Domestics, Dress, Diseases, and Descendants.* It is a good, rule-of-thumb list, though I believe that there is no topic of conversation that is boring per se. It takes a bore to make it boring, and being a bore is usually the mere calamity of miscalculating one's audience, a thing for which some people have a more marked talent than others.

Miscalculation of this sort makes bores of even the

* A variant of this cliché described the woman whose conversation was "bounded on the north by her servants, on the west by her children, on the south by her ailments, and on the east by her clothes."

most brilliant men and the most charming women, and it is the very qualities that make them fascinating to some people in some circumstances that make them dull or obtuse to other people in other circumstances. George Bernard Shaw was once voted the greatest bore in England at a time when his countrymen found his acidity out of date and his warnings unnecessary. There is a simple way to explain this. La Rochefoucauld in his *Maxims* said, "We often pardon those who bore us, but never those whom we bore," and presumably the British could not forgive Mr. Shaw for being bored with them.

It is a wise man who knows whom he bores. But by this same token there is no such thing as a boring person, and there is no person who is not a bore. The bore, like beauty, exists only in the eye of the beholder, for the bore, alas, is from within.

III. Weekend Guests

IF YOU have a house on an upland meadow, or a cottage by the sea, or a cabin in the woods, you are likely to discover by the middle of June that the precious relaxation which you have waited out the winter to enjoy is a mirage. The weekends during which you intended to commune with nature and your family are booked solid with weekend guests until after Labor Day. You have nothing but your own hospitable nature and your social conscientiousness to blame.

To those who are naturally hospitable, weekend guests in the abstract are nearly always attractive. They call to mind hospitality of a leisurely sort, and that in turn reminds us of pleasant hours we have spent in our own houses and the houses of friends—afternoons active in the sun or dozing in the shade, amiable meals and

34

comfortable beds, breakfasts out of doors with grass-hoppers whirring in the nearby meadow, log fires on nights still with snow. It is a picture of enchantment,

One of the noblest things that a weekend has to recommend it is that sooner, rather than later, it is over.

but when weekend guests become specific, and nostalgia is translated into problems of towels and food and personalities, we grow concerned. Even if our anticipation is happy, we are aware as our guests approach that one of the noblest things that a weekend has to recommend it is that sooner, rather than later, it is over.

If you are a part-time country dweller you have almost certainly managed during the winter to accumulate obligations that seemed easy to put off until summer when you could repay them with interest. Sometimes the invitations you dispense are your own idea; sometimes you are the victim of those who don't think it is worth their while to find themselves a haven in the country, so long as they have friends who have gone to that trouble for them. These are the people who are quick to inquire about your country place and to whom you mutter with general affability, "You must come out and see us sometime." Before you have clamped your lips shut on this treacherous cliché, they are thumbing through their engagement books, and you are committed for the third weekend in July—"or if that's not convenient, what about the first weekend in August?"

For the most part, however, you have acted of your own free will, and you have carved the image of your summer with your own hands. Not all weekend guests are problems, of course; otherwise they and the custom of inviting them would long ago have fallen into disuse. The odds, indeed, are well on the side of your urging only those you know you are going to enjoy to share your hospitality. What makes a good guest is a subtle complex of personality, manners, and delicacy of feeling, coupled with one's own state of forbearance at the moment when the guest appears. There are friends one can always depend on, but they are likely to be old friends for whom no amount of trouble is a burden and whose awareness of one's shortcomings is equaled by their readiness to accept them.

But not all guests can be old friends; they are merely the certain islands of calm and delight in a summer filled with potential catastrophe. Let us consider those other guests, most of whom we have invited in over-expansive moments to share our hospitality.

The standard weekend guests are a couple, but there the standard stops and the variations set in. We cannot discuss all of the variations, but let us take a few common ones, and their children, and face up to this problem before it is too late to do anything about it, which it almost surely will be.

Age makes less difference in guests than you would think; it is "habit patterns" (as the psychologists call the ruts of behavior) that are important to consider in dealing with guests. If, for example, you have invited what seemed to you on urban acquaintance a lively, active couple, you may as well resign yourself to their spending most of the weekend asleep. Being lively in the city is an extremely enervating business, and your couple will make up for it over the weekend. There is no use leaving the lawnmower conspicuously displayed; these are not the kind of people who are going to volunteer to push it. The chances are that they will arrive late for dinner on Friday completely equipped for tennis, golf, and swimming, and it will take the whole family to stow them and their tack in the guest room. By nine o'clock one of them will say: "Oh, this country air. I can hardly keep my eyes open." And by nine-thirty they'll both be asleep, or something, upstairs.

On Saturday morning it becomes obvious that these active urban types are country sluggards. They emerge dressed like manikins from a resort shop—the man in slacks and loafers and plaid shirt and his wife in shorts and sandals and halter—in the clothes, in other words, that people who spend much time in the country haven't time for—and they wear dark glasses. If you are sensible, you have been up for a good while yourself and got the lawn mowed (your guests love to lie in bed and listen to the reassuring whir of a lawnmower) and had your breakfast. You have made a list of the things you want to do without regard to what your friends want to do. If they feel like it they'll patter along when you go to town to shop; if they don't, they are perfectly happy sitting in reclining chairs, their faces lifted like platters to the sun. You need not worry about all the sports equipment they brought with them. That was a gesture. They won't begin to bustle until late afternoon when it is cocktail time. Then they will replace their shorts with something longer, and emerge after they have used up all the hot water, ready to use up all the gin.

The chances of what may then happen are about equally divided; they may drink so fast and furiously (they feel so full of health from a day in the sun) that they will again be ready for bed by nine-thirty. If this happens, Sunday's performance will echo Saturday's. If, however, they decide to make an evening of it, they won't appear until just before lunch on Sunday, by which time you can have had at least a half a day to yourself. The rest of the day you may as well throw away.

By contrast, let us look at a quite different sort of couple from the city. It would be risking too much to say that the opposite type, the kind of couple who reflect the cares and the harrying tempo of urban life and have a peaked air about them, are invariably the active ones over a weekend in the country, but there is some truth in it. They are likely to arrive somewhat bedraggled, usually by train, with the hot sooty look of people emerging from a couple of hours on a local in which the air conditioning has broken down. The first breath of clear country air brightens their gray faces; they stand on the platform and look around them as though refreshing their memories of what a tree looks like. They have a small suitcase each and carry no athletic equipment. If everything about the landscape enchants them as you drive them home, you should be warned that you are in for an active two days.

This sort of couple has a good deal in common with puppies. You throw out any kind of suggestion, and they scamper after it and bring it back and drop it at your feet. Everything is grist for their mill, but they have forgotten to bring the mill. If you suggest tennis, they'd just love tennis, but, of course, they have no rackets and no sneakers, and after you have ransacked the house and tried your own, your wife's, and your children's sneakers on them and have concluded that you are in for a game of pat-ball, they settle down to beat the pants off you with rackets that you have long since given up as warped and worthless.

You can save up the lawn for this type. One will surely cut it for you while the other weeds the flowers, or they may work in shifts. You will have difficulty keeping them out of the kitchen, if you are the sort who thinks of the kitchen as your private sanctum, because they will insist on helping with the dishes. The only real trouble you will encounter arises if you are so mis-guided as to leave them to their own devices to entertain themselves. Their puppy eyes will look at you as though you ought to be throwing a ball for them. You even have to suggest to them that it is time to go to bed. When you put them on the train on Sunday evening, you will notice that for all the healthful paces through which they have put you and themselves, they will have that same gray and harried look they had when they arrived.

These two kinds of couples are, of course, merely composites of many other species. But what of the couples who do not seem to make pairs and who go their separate ways? And what of those couples of which you like one member and can't abide the other? For our purposes they

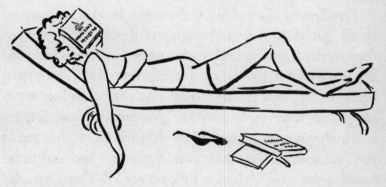

"Don't bother about me; I can take care of myself."

have to be considered as individuals. There are those who think that the state of being a guest relieves them of all responsibility and those who consider guesthood a perpetual challenge. In either case the extremes are difficult to cope with.

The range of individual guests is, of course, endless, and perforce we must confine ourselves to those whose eccentricities have some chance of seeming to be part of larger and more universally recognized patterns. You can make your own synthesis (nobody is anybody these days who doesn't at least try to make a synthesis) and match them as you please.

Some guests want to be left alone, and some say they want to ("Don't bother about me. Just go about your business. I'll find plenty to do.") and are miserable if they are.

The first of these lone wolves can be the pleasantest of all guests if they are resourceful, can take care of themselves happily, and at the same time pervade your household with the warm feeling that they enjoy just being in it. At their best they don't mind being interrupted in their own pursuits if there is some activity in which you want them to join. At their worst they make you feel that all they want out of you is a bed and three meals a day and a chance to ignore you. These are the men and women who come for the weekend to get away from people (including you) and to have a little quiet. They think they have discharged all of their responsibilities if they bring a box of chocolates that they have bought in the railroad station. They are so well able to take care of themselves that they make you feel as though you were in their employ.

A guest of the second type (who really does not want to be left alone but protests that he does) offers an acute problem of tact. He appears at breakfast with a small stack of books, a magazine, and some writing paper, bright-eyed and presumably equipped for the day. He quickly sets the books aside and takes your morning paper. (The sort of person who has a number of books from which to choose is rarely a reader. He is always looking for a chance to find some time to sit down with a good book, but curiously he never seems to find it. He won't find it over the weekend either.) After his third cup of coffee, you may get back the paper, and your friend will wander off to find a place to read one of the books. In half an hour or less he'll be hovering around again. "Too nice a day to sit and read," he'll say, and that is your signal to quit whatever you are doing and invent something to keep him busy. His resources and imagination were exhausted by picking out which books in your library he would fondle.

If this type stretches your tact, then you should be especially warned of the guest who makes an elaborate show of being tactful about you. He acts as though he knows that he is too much trouble and that everything you do for him is a great nuisance. He is constantly leaping out of his chair to perform some little service for you or for your wife, to get out the ice, to find the children's ball in the bushes, or to fetch the wood for the fireplace, all of which would be ingratiating if it weren't done half-apologetically. You soon find yourself wanting to tell him to sit down and relax, but instead you respond with an elaborate display of tact on your own part. He is wearisome because he is so hard to live up to.

Even so he is preferable to the intentionally tactless guest who thinks that to make light of your shortcomings as a host is a demonstration of easy fellowship and poise. He laughs at the way you lay a fire, and insists on taking your effort apart and stacking the kindling in his way. He reminds you that the leaky faucet in the bathroom could be fixed with a five-cent washer and fifteen min-utes' work, and that you have put the wrong kind of composition shingles on your house; he could have got a much better brand for you wholesale at half the price you paid. He follows you wherever you go all weekend long; he stands in the kitchen door while you are getting drinks or a meal. If you play golf with him he tells you how to correct your slice, and if he sees you chopping wood he will observe that you are lucky you haven't cut your leg off long since, handling an axe the way you do. When he is not telling you how you ought to live, his conversation is almost entirely about the remarkable place at which he spent last weekend, with friends who did everything in such style. He is unaware that the walls of most country places are excellent conductors of sound, and you have no respite from him for some time after he has presumably gone to bed. If he is married, you can listen to him telling his wife that you would have a nice little place if you only knew how to take care of it.

Even the careless guest is preferable to the tactless type, though he too offers some minor aggravations. He

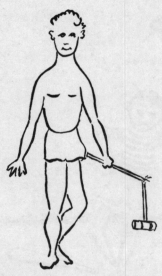

The careless guest—there's no malice in his soul, though, and it is possible to love him.

strews the place with his belongings, he breaks a blade of the lawnmower on a rock anyone ought to be able to see, and he invariably is inspired to take a dip in the lake or river or ocean just as you are about to produce lunch or supper. When he does ultimately appear to be fed he will have deposited his wet bathing suit over the back of a piece of upholstered furniture. There is no malice in his soul though, and it is possible to love him.

It is impossible, on the other hand, to love the belligerently indolent guest who frustrates all attempts to

The reply is invariably, "Not particularly."

make his visit pleasant or interesting. That is not to say that a host should force entertainment on anyone who doesn't want it, for a good host knows when to put enticements in his guest's way and when not to. But the belligerently indolent guest has a gift for making it quite obvious to his host that he expects to be entertained, yet displays a distinct distaste for any diversion that may be suggested to him. This is a common characteristic in children, and in adults it is, I believe, an indication of retarded maturity. I have often seen adults behave like a child I know who continually asks, "What'll I do now?" When a suggestion is made to him he has a pat reply. "Would you like to go swimming?" you ask him, and the reply is invariably, "Not particularly." "Well then," you say trying again, "how would you like to play catch?" "Not particularly," he says, and so it goes. When such guests, children or adults, do finally submit themselves to some plan you have suggested, they give you the uncomfortable sensation that they wish you had been bright enough to invent something really entertaining.

If this kind of guest is tiring because he is a constant challenge to your ingenuity, the opposite type, the ebullient guest, who sets out to give his host and hostess a rousing good time, takes the least planning and is the most exhausting. He arrives full of ideas, of projects for excursions, of resolve to get you out and give you some real exercise, and unless you want to be rude to him (which is necessary in extreme cases) it is best just to put yourself in his hands.

There are a number of common manifestations of the ebullient guest, each requiring a special defensive operation and its own system of logistics. I happen to have a house in the Berkshires. These gentle hills were at one time (especially in the environs of Stockbridge and Lenox) remarkable for the size and extravagance of the summer estates which graced their slopes. There is a legend in the Berkshires that a young man who was at Yale just before the turn of the century sent his mother a telegram in which he said, "BRINGING SOME '97 FRIENDS FOR WEEKEND," and his mother wired back, "TERRIBLY SORRY HAVE ROOM FOR ONLY SEVENTY-SIX." Most of the big estates are now hotels, or schools, or church institutions, and the Berkshires have become a hotbed of summer culture. We have music festivals at Tanglewood that rival Salzburg and Glyndebourne in fame. We have dance festivals at a place called Jacob's Pillow, and we have enough summer theaters to give several platoons of Broadway stars their annual breath of fresh air. We used to frequent these places; in fact months before the music festival our friends could be seen conspicuously angling for invitations. We finally grew tired of running a lodging house for our music- and dance-minded acquaintances, and we ourselves took to angling for invitations elsewhere during that part of the summer. It was the ebullient guests who wanted to be sure that we got our dosage of culture who finally drove us to take umbrage.

Umbrage is one way to cope with the ebullient. Another way is to lend your guests the family car, and if necessary your wife, and let them go on an excursion of their own making. A third method is to buy two tickets to the festival or the dance or the theater and say that they are all you could get (which could easily be true) and insist that the guests use them. This is both a generous gesture and assurance of a few hours' respite.

There is one kind of ebullience, however, which I have frequently encountered and have never been able to discover an answer to. It is found in a single guest or in a couple who seem to know a great many more people in the vicinity to which you have invited them than you do. The minute they get in the house they start calling up their friends. By the end of fifteen minutes they have invited themselves and you to one house for lunch, another for drinks, and have possibly even got you committed to appear at the Saturday night country club dance. You may, on the other hand, find yourself giving a cocktail party for a lot of people you scarcely know and have been successfully avoiding for years. Short of cutting the telephone wires before your guests arrive, I know of no way to keep their socially manic behavior in control.

There are, of course, many other types of weekend guests than these few I have mentioned, especially the perfect guests, of whom there are as many varieties as there are of imperfect ones, but before we leave those of our contemporaries who strain the muscles of our hospitality, and turn our attention to their offspring, I should like to mention a matter of utmost concern to hostesses—food.

There is, for example, the problem of breakfast. What does a hostess do about those guests who insist that she just leave a pot of coffee on the stove and they'll have a cup whenever they get up? They don't mean it of course; what they really want is a full breakfast at the moment when they have drained away the last bit of sleep, whether it is at nine or eleven-thirty, and they would really like it brought to them in bed.

One of the accepted conventions in this age of relaxed hospitality is the privilege of sleeping late on weekends, and while the guests sleep the routine of the household founders. The children have to be kept quiet, the kitchen can be only partly cleaned up, the day's plans must wait. If you could take your guests a tray at any specific hour, then planning would be possible, but no. You are much more likely to be faced with a guest who emerges just before lunch and to wonder whether you should offer him a martini or a soft-boiled egg.

People who go visiting in the country look forward to the casual life, and they assume that this means that meals just happen whenever it is convenient for them. They show up when and as they please just as surely for lunch or dinner as for breakfast, and expect that some magic will have produced a cold collation or a hot meal.

If they are on elaborate diets, such as the salt-free or bland, then meals become to them the most important occasion of the day and also the most embarrassing. Diets are not nearly so hard for a hostess to deal with as the apologies with which they are accompanied. Some years ago I arrived at the house of a friend for the weekend

Should you offer him a martini or a soft-boiled egg?

with a case of cream soups and puréed vegetables which I produced with an elaborate apology for the unfortunate state of my viscera. "That's quite all right," my hostess reassured me, "but don't let me hear you apologize once more or I'll feed this pap to the cat."

The best measure of any guest is his attitude toward your children. It may be that they are brats, and you know it and momentarily you are not proud of them. You may be ashamed of their manners or their dirty faces or their fresh remarks, or of their shyness or cussedness, or of whatever phase they may presently be exhibiting. But the ways in which your guests react to them will tell you more about your friends than any other social litmus paper.

Children (it is hard for adults to remember) have their own kind of dignity, and they find many adults ridiculously childish, or perhaps I should say ridiculously grown-up. It is the guests who make your children feel younger than they are or not worth bothering with who should be avoided. The ones who treat them as people are rare. They are at least as rare as the children who behave themselves when you have guests around.

But what about children as guests? It is axiomatic that children when visiting without their parents behave better than they do either at home or when their parents go visiting with them. When they are on their own, there is nobody to whom they can shift the responsibility for their behavior; when they are visiting with their parents they take a special delight in being outrageous because they know they have the upper hand. From experience they have learned that a parent who will lose his temper at them at home can be counted on to make no such display in somebody else's house. They know too that a child who misbehaves in public is "the parents' fault." Where they get this idea, I do not know; but they get it early and use it for all it is worth.

Children who are usually obedient at home (or at least can be reasoned with) turn out to be little furies when they come visiting with their parents over a weekend. They show off; they sulk; they make a fuss about going to bed. Worst of all they get up at the crack of dawn and bounce a ball against the house just below your bedroom window. They don't like the food. They either are afraid of your dog and cringe whenever he appears, or they pull his tail and make him growl, so that either way you have no choice but to lock him in the cellar. Normally resourceful children when visiting can never think of anything to do, and like the child whose refrain was "Not particularly" they delight in straining your imagination and patience by finding all of your suggestions a stupendous bore. If you have children of your own, the juvenile sense of rivalry quickly sets up tensions which often burst into open warfare, and your children always get the blame because they are not being good little hosts and hostesses.

Possibly more difficult than young children are visiting teen-agers, who, unless you have prearranged a schedule of activities for them, hang around and are a constant and constantly bored rebuke. They have arrived at the age when they no longer think that adults are sophisticated and are beginning to wonder how anybody over thirty manages to drag his aging body around. The games of childhood are behind them, and the games that adults enjoy are stuffy. They are always full of animal spirits and animal lethargy; they are always on their

guard lest they should allow a telltale crack to appear in their façade of sophistication, mortally afraid that they may say or do something that might appear naïve. If, however, it is possible to arrange for them to join a group of their contemporaries, you are likely to be rid of them,

* In this connection it is interesting to note that it is characteristic of visiting dogs always to want to be on the side of the screen door on which they are not.

so entirely rid of them that you may wonder whether you shouldn't be taking your responsibilities more seriously.

If you will refer to Stevenson's *Home Book of Quotations,* as I often do when I am looking for an epigram, you will find that an author named Laboulaye in a book called *Abdullah* said: "The first day a man is a guest, the second a burden, the third a pest."

The weekend is so devised that only a few guests stay around until they are pests.* Counting the day as twenty-

* Not only Laboulaye had this time-concept of guests. For those who like documentation for its own sake,† here are some variants on the theme, starting with the Roman playright Plautus (about 200 B.C.) who said: "No guest is so welcome that he will not become a nuisance after three days in a friend's house."‡

Seventeen centuries later John Lyly made a fashionable switch by crediting the idea to the Greeks. He also added a gustatorial note, which stuck. In the *Euphues* (1580) he wrote: "As we say in Athens, fishe and gesse [guests] in three days are stale."

Other writers who have used this same figure of speech (and who probably thought they invented it) include Robert Herrick ("Two days y'ave landed here; a third yee know, Makes guests and fish smell strong; pray go." *Hesperides,* 1684) and Benjamin Franklin, who couldn't leave the idea alone. In 1733 he wrote: "After three days men grow weary of a wench, a guest, and rainy weather." Three years later he had boiled it down to "Fish and company smell in three days."

By the nineteenth century the phrase had been vulgarized to: "Fish and company stink in three days." And not longer ago than 1938 S. G. Champion in a book called *Racial Proverbs* cites a Japanese proverb: "Fish and guests are wearisome on

four hours (though it may seem like more) and assuming
that most weekend guests arrive on Friday evening, they
usually sit out the "burden" period and leave just before
the "pest" period sets in. The occasional extension of the
weekend to 6:00 A.M. on Monday,* when those who
want to avoid the Sunday night traffic tiptoe out of the
house like a herd of buffalo, fortifies Laboulaye's aphor-
ism, but there are some guests who leave when they are
still only burdens and becomes pests *in absentia*.

I do not mean merely those who go off with the Sunday paper (at which you have not had a chance) in order
to have something to read on the train, or those who have
stowed in their suitcases the detective story that you (as
well as they) have half read. I mean those who, snail-

---

the third day." There is no evidence that Benjamin Franklin
had ever been to Japan.

Considering the chronological span of these quotations and
their wide geographical distribution, they evidence a consistency
of thought about guests which overrides the barriers of cultures
and time. Modern refrigeration has licked the fish problem;
it is unlikely that anyone will ever lick the guest problem.

† Lest anyone consider this an unwarranted display of
scholarship on the part of the author, he is referred to page
1045 of the 1948 edition of Stevenson's compendium, where
he will find all of these references.

‡ Freely translated this means: "Nam hospes nullus tam in
amici hospitium devorti potest, Quin, ubi tridoum continuom
fuerit, iam odiosus siet."

* The *Vogue Book of Etiquette* says that it is to be taken
for granted that the weekend lasts until Monday morning. Not
at my house.

like, leave a sticky trail behind them. They are often the ones who say as they get on the train or pull out of the driveway, "If I've left anything behind, just throw it away."

What they have left behind is usually a tennis racket, putter, scooter, or other ungainly object that is impossible to throw away and defies being sent by parcel post or even by express without the most elaborate crating. Toothbrushes, razors, compacts, handkerchiefs, socks, lipsticks are easily forgotten by the departed guest, but if the object is really awkward, you will know at once that it will be badly missed. Monday night will bring a phone call full of self-accusation and urgency.

It is sometimes with a sense of loss, but more often with a sense of relief that one speeds the parting weekender, no matter how pleasant the visit may have been. If the weekend has been a success from everyone's point of view, it is just as well that enthusiasm cannot be stretched to the point where it diminishes to mere amicability, or amicability to the point where it becomes tolerance. If it was a good weekend, the quiet that the guests leave behind them is filled with pleasant echoes of the always unfinished business of friendship. If it has not been good, then they take away with them the burdensome business which has kept you struggling for the last forty-eight hours.

And this most surely explains the weekend as an

institution. Its duration has been set by convention; the
end is always in view and never very far away. The most
dreary guests can be tolerated and coped with for forty-
eight hours, and the most pleasant ones can be relished
without fear that the pleasure of their presence will
diminish. It was a wise host who invented the weekend,
a host with a most sensitively balanced appreciation of
the limits of man's social appetite and especially of his
social endurance.

IV. Hosts and Hostesses

SINCE the dawn of the Republic, books of etiquette, hundreds of different ones, have been avidly consumed by Americans. Social conditions and the amenities considered necessary to meet them have, of course, changed immeasurably since the days when we were an upstart nation which patterned its drawing-room manners on those of England and France. Early in the last century, eating with the knife was considered quite proper so long as one didn't close the lips tightly over the blade, and the time is not long past when it was necessary to advise guests not to let their hostesses know "that you have found or felt insects in your bed." Books of manners used to be complete guides for the socially uncertain (and who could be certain in a time when manners were so elaborate and changing so rapidly?), but now we have entered an era of specialization even in informality, and there are special guides to particular social amenities.

You can, for example, learn the art of entertaining for twenty-five cents and the application of some diligence by purchasing a copy of a little book called *You, Too, Can Be the Perfect Hostess*. I found my copy in a stationery and cigar store. You, too, can find your copy in a stationery and cigar store when you drop in to buy some decalcomania burlesque girls to decorate your highball glasses or some multicolored pencils and pads for hilarious pencil and paper games. There are a mere two hundred and eighty pages between you and being the perfect hostess, or, if you are a man, to find out how drab your life has been.

With such a complete and inexpensive guide readily available, it may seem presumptuous of me to train my inadequate guns on a field which has already been subjected to saturation bombardment by a professional who is so thoroughly at home among the tea and scones. But I have been trying to picture myself and my friends at some of the parties suggested to the potentially perfect hostess, and I feel myself inching toward the door for a breath of fresh air. I think, therefore, that we should look briefly at this proposed road to perfection.

The introduction to *You, Too, Can Be the Perfect*

Hostess stresses two aspects of social deportment which are at odds with what I was brought up to believe were the fundamentals of hospitality. "A husband and wife," the author says, "who turn a backyard steak fry into a

"You can put personality (your own) into a party and cut costs accordingly."

festive occasion are building security for themselves in a social, personal, and business sense." The other sentence which caught my eye was this: "You can put personality (your own) into a party and cut costs accordingly."

Consider the steak fry. If you couple the festival idea
with cost-cutting, what you are likely to get is a very
large dose of personality and practically no fried steak.
It is, however, unquestionably this attitude which has
caused the appearance of chef's caps and comic aprons
in the backyards of the nation. No amount of personality
(genuine or bought in bar marts) is going to make a
piece of fried steak on which you have cut costs any less
tough, and I doubt if it would build security, social,
personal, or business, either.

It is not fair to dwell on a couple of carelessly written
sentences like these, because once the reader gets well
into the pages of *You, Too,* it fairly bounces with good
humor, and the venal aspects of hospitality, though
never quite forgotten, become obscured in a dazzling
display of imaginative fancies. You have no idea how
far from perfect you are until you have read the chapters
on how to give a "Sadie Hawkins Day" or a "Doggie
Roast" or a "Come-as-you-were-the-night-he-proposed
Masquerade" party.

According to the author, the invitation to the last of
these festivals should read:

> *How did he look, what did you see . . .*
> *The night he asked, "Won't you marry me?"*
> *Come in "authentic costume."*

The invitation to another form of gaiety, a "Gay-Nineties Party," we are told, should be "written in white ink on red paper pasted with a border of red and white rickrack," and it should start with the admonition: "Hop on your bicycle built for two. . . ."

According to the publisher's blurb on the cover of *You, Too* this is all part of the "new, easy, relaxed way to entertain," and the author of this social treatise, Maureen Daly, is billed as "the leading expert on modern manners." In the face of such easy relaxation and such authority I find myself growing tense.

I don't think I have received an invitation written on red paper in white ink and set about with rickrack since I got out of the seventh grade, and if even figuratively hopping on a bicycle built for two is the price I must pay for modern manners, I am certainly not living in the same era with Miss Daly,* and so am not equipped to deal with this delicate subject of hosts and hostesses. It just makes me want to lie down for twenty minutes, as *Vogue* recommends that hostesses do, with cold pads over my eyes and see if I can get rid of my crow's feet.†

There is another manual, however, that I find much more sympathetic. It is called *The Illustrated Manners*

---

* According to her publishers, Miss Daly is still in her twenties, and "knows how the new generation lives."

† *Vogue* may not have recommended this, but the reader will agree that it is the sort of thing that *Vogue* would recommend if they thought of it.

Book, a Manual of Good Behavior and Polite Accomplishments, and it was published in New York in 1855. I was attracted to it first by an item in a chapter called "Of Various Relations" which reads:

. . . There is another class of professional people we sometimes encounter in society, and the proper treatment of them may be a matter of consideration. We mean authors, editors, artists, musicians, &c. These people, with the exception, perhaps, of editors, are apt to be sensitive, irritable, and *exigeant.* They are to be treated with corresponding delicacy. . . .

Obviously here is a writer of sensibility who stresses culture (indeed he devotes a chapter to it) and doesn't play around with such oddments as "Potluck Supper, United Nations Style" and "Easter Brunch" the way Miss Daly does. In fact he thinks that my kind should be treated with delicacy, and so, indeed, do I. Furthermore he is a man of principles. He recognizes that a man may be "sensitive, irritable, and *exigeant*" and still warrant the consideration of a hostess and her other guests. Miss Daly in her book, on the other hand, when discussing the subject of games says, ". . . ignore the shy and backward guests and start things moving."

One of the things that would start moving would be the authors, editors, musicians, &c., if I know them, and their direction could not be controlled by the hostess.

All of the manners books into which I have looked

agree unanimously on one essential characteristic of the good hostess—she must not be nervous. This, it seems to me, is a fallacy. When my hostess isn't nervous, I am. That is not to say that she should display her fidgets, but if she hasn't the wit to know that a party is a multiple

The Nervous Hostess

man-trap set about with *oubliettes* and that she owes it to her guests to be nervous about the state of their well-being, then I would rather have stayed at home. The hostess who is perfectly sure of herself and at ease lacks imagination and is either bossy or fades into her company like just another guest.

65

Let us look for a moment at some of the kinds of hostesses we are likely to encounter and at some hosts as well. It is essentially they and not the guests who set the tone of modern hospitality. If there is blame or praise to be distributed for the degree to which we enjoy or dislike to be entertained, it rightfully falls upon the perpetrators not on the recipients of hospitality.

First, let's take the bossy hostess whom we have just mentioned. She is not uncommon. Instead of waiting like a general for a mishap to reveal her genius, she makes her guests constantly aware that they are pawns in a game of strategy. Her gifts are more executive than social, and she has never learned to distinguish between them. She approaches a party in her own house as though she were madam chairman of a convention hospitality committee, and she sees to it that everyone does his or her job. Her function in her own eyes is to "make things go." And go they do. There is never a dull moment, nor a moment of relaxation either. No sooner are you settled in conversation with someone than you are whisked away to talk to someone else on the assumption that in this parallel to musical chairs no one is going to get stuck with anyone and nobody will be bored. Nobody will be bored, perhaps, but nearly everyone will be frustrated.

There is a quality about the bossy hostess that reminds one of children's parties at which there is always an

Some hostesses act as though they were madam chairnan of a convention hospitality committee.

adult to see that things get started and that when the initial silence is finally overcome they don't get out of hand.

When I was about eleven my father moved away from New England to a new parish, and my mother gave a party for me in the rectory, a real dinner party for about a dozen boys and girls of my own age none of whom I knew. I had been away at school, and these were the sons and daughters of parishioners. They were as becalmed by being deposited at the rectory by their parents as I was awe-struck at the prospect of facing a strange, new crowd of my contemporaries. I think that the first ten minutes of that dinner were the most uneasy of my childhood. Not a word was said. The soup came and went in deadly silence. The girls sat stiffly in their party dresses, and the boys tugged at their Eton collars. Then my father appeared in the door of the dining room (he was always suspicious of quiet children). "Anything the matter?" he asked. Everyone looked around at him, but no one said anything. He made a joke of some sort and none of the children laughed. "Well," he said, "have a good time," and wisely retired. Then after another minute, silence, as if blown away by a gust of wind, was gone, and the first symptoms of what ended in near pandemonium swept happily around the table.

A hostess with a firm but unthreatening hand and a

gift for planning is essential to a children's party, but the wise hostess realizes that at a party for any age it is not generalship that matters but sensitiveness to the mood of the group. My father's little joke, which fell so flat that I cannot remember it, was enough to make the children forget their self-consciousness for the split second that was needed to uncork their bottled spirits.

The bossy hostess, being unimaginative, has got to be administrative. Having no talent for either compromise or improvisation, she has made her plans long in advance and she brooks no interference with them. If her guests have no taste for what she has devised to keep them entertained she is unaware of it. She is so absorbed in her own strategy that she has no idea what goes on in anyone's mind but her own. She directs the conversation at dinner; she arranges whom you will talk with after dinner, and she insists that you make a fool of yourself at some game you have carefully avoided learning how to play.

By contrast the hostess who moves among her guests like a disembodied spirit resigns all responsibility for what happens. She is quite sure that she has done her part by seeing to it that there is food and drink and that a certain number of people have forgathered, and having done that, she means to sit back and enjoy herself. She becomes a guest at her own party. If the party dies on its feet, which parties are likely to do when no one is taking the initiative for them, she blames her guests for not having seen to it that she had more fun. Fortunately for such hostesses and her friends there is usually someone who steps in and assumes an unobtrusive role of leadership.

The bossy hostess and the woman who acts like a guest in her own house are extremes, though unfortunately not uncommon ones. Somewhere between them are a variety of types who haven't got matters in hand but would like to and are so afraid that their hospitality is going to fall apart at any minute that they communicate their own mild hysteria to their friends.

The apologetic hostess is one of these. She calls you on the phone and pleads: "I do hope you'll come," she says. "It's going to be terribly dull: just old friends, no interesting people. Come and help cheer it up." The flattery implied in the last statement isn't enough to offset your suspicion that her prognosis is probably quite accurate. Your sympathy, however, has been elicited and you accept. The apologies are by no means over. You arrive to be greeted by your hostess with some such statement as: "I tried to make the drinks myself, and I'm afraid they're dreadful," and you leave to the accompaniment of: "You were terribly nice to come. I'm dreadfully ashamed that dinner was so utterly tasteless and that everyone sat around like lumps afterward."

Dinner, of course, had been a most elaborate production and the company had seemed excellent.

It is one thing to put up with this sort of mock-apologetic behavior for an evening, but to have to devote a weekend to reassuring a perfectly competent hostess is sticky. How many times has one encountered a hostess who apologizes for the reading light in the bedroom, the noises the children make, the mosquitoes, the lack of sheen on the silver, the lack of bluing in the linen, the condition of the flower beds, the greens on the golf course, even the crowing of a rooster a quarter of a mile down the road which she is sure must have waked you at dawn? There are only just so many variations that one can play on the theme, "Why, not at all. I think it's lovely." Eventually even the richest imagination balks.

Men are less likely to betray an apologetic attitude than women; they do not feel called upon to display their pride by devious methods but are content to use the direct attack. "Let me show you around the place," a country host will say before you have got your city clothes off and your face washed. You head for the barn, and if he has cows you are invited to examine their udders and a chart that gives the yield and butterfat count of each cow and you will learn how much Sweetsop Lilypad of Blueshire cost at what auction. On the way out you are introduced to the compost pile, a marvel of nature at work recreating herself, and you are invited to plunge your hand into it to see for yourself how much heat it generates. Whether you know or care anything about cows and compost is no matter; you'll know more before you get through, even if you care less.

I was once taken out to the woodshed by my host before I had got my bags out of the car because he had just that morning devised a sort of filing system for his firewood. He had divided it up into three sections: breakfast wood (very light dry kindling and cedar because it makes a hot, fast fire), luncheon wood (birch mostly, because it burns fairly fast and crackles happily), and dinner wood (mainly apple because it will last through a long evening). He was very proud of it, but I would have been happier to look at it if I had had a chance to pull myself together a bit first.

There is something reassuring about this kind of immediate enthusiasm. This sort of host not infrequently gets his pride of proprietorship out of his system in the first few hours of your visit, and from then on the pace slackens and you are allowed to go about your business of relaxation much as you please.

Certainly he is to be preferred to the weekend host or hostess who has planned every minute of your time from the moment you open your eyes to the stillness of a country morning until you close your throbbing lids many exhausting hours later. When you are in the hands of

those who are uncomfortable unless every minute is
accounted for, you are told at breakfast what your day
will be like, and the day's schedule reads like the menu
of a seven-course blue-plate dinner—and no substitu-
tions:

Appetizer
Trip to village to pick up daily paper

First Course
(Choice of one) Golf foursome (mixed) *or* sitting
on club porch

Second Course
Picnic lunch by roaring brook,
beer cooled in stream

Third Course
Twenty-five mile drive to Antique Shoppe to
pick up needlework motto to hang over fireplace. Route by way of "view"

Fourth Course
Swim at lake cottage of friends of hosts,
followed by beer cooled in lake

Fifth Course
Cocktails at lake cottage next door to friends
of hosts. Unlimited choice of uncooked vegetables, sun-tanned women, and small children

73

Sixth Course

Picnic by roaring fire, beer cooled in ice buckets

Seventh Course

Edward Everett Horton in *Springtime for
Henry* at Olde Loft Playhouse

Dessert

Pick up Hostess's children at Square Dance. Coca-Cola

And then you may sit up half the night going over in
detail the things you did all day and dissecting the
people you played golf and drank with. There are of
course as many variants to this menu as there are over-
conscientious hosts and hostesses.

It is as fruitless to try to buck the regimented weekend or party as it is to try to make order out of the
plans of the hostess who has so many minds of her own
that she can't make up any of them. She is so eager
to see that you aren't bored that she has devised a
series of alternate amusements which she flings at you
like a handful of ping-pong balls. Your inclination is
to duck, but your sense of social responsibility makes
you grab first at this one and then at that, with the
result that all of them slip through your fingers. You
leave your hostess with the impression that you are
impossible to amuse.

This sort of bird-shot planning which is meant to eject

74

so many little pellets that some of them must wing the guests is a far cry from the stereotyped methods of entertainment that our grandparents knew in the days when the rules of each kind of party were rigidly defined. The general disintegration of formality has put more of a burden on most hosts and hostesses than

We live in an age of potluck.

they are able to assume with equanimity. The result is to find artificial ways to make people seem relaxed, or if they are naturally relaxed to emphasize their most ludicrous qualities. Relaxation has gone a good deal further than even Miss Daly would think suitable.

We live in the age of potluck, the era of "You'll have to take us as you find us." The household in which the turn is called by the servants is a vanishing institution. There are comparatively few homes these days in which the hostess is intimidated into rushing her guests through their drinks because she is frightened of the disapprobation of the cook if dinner is delayed for ten minutes. The complexity of life "below stairs" is not what it was a generation or two ago. There is no longer the sense in most establishments that somewhere out of sight there is a well-ordered world with a political system all its own that is going to burst into open revolt if its rights are flouted by the disturbance of its schedule.

The casserole has taken the place of the seven-course dinner, and the living-in servant has been replaced by a woman who comes in by the hour or by nobody at all. Dinner happens whenever the hostess decides that her guests have the fidgets. She disappears and reappears at intervals. She announces the approach of food as though it were a race horse rounding the turn and coming into the stretch. "Just another couple of minutes," she says, and then finally after half an hour has passed: "It's ready whenever you are."

Potluck is not limited to meals. What the casserole, with its meat and vegetables and gravy all stewed together with spices, is to the formal dinner, the potluck household is to the formal household of another day. "Just come any time," your hostess says. "This is Liberty Hall." If you can stomach that one, and you do show up, let's say for a weekend, you are likely to encounter not only potluck but bedluck and find yourself stowed away on the sleeping porch with a four-year-old who wakes up at six and pretends that his bed is a foxhole and that he is fighting the Battle of the Bulge with sound effects. You come down to what you hope will be breakfast (not quite literally shot to pieces) to find that you and the boy who has his orders to stay in the foxhole are the only ones awake. Last night's debris—half-filled glasses, chock-full ashtrays—bedecks the living room and the kitchen sink is filled with dishes, "left to soak." But you set out to find where your hostess hides the coffee. When you discover it in a canister marked SUGAR, you dump last night's grounds into the sink (so as not to seem like a fussy housekeeper in this carefree atmosphere). Then in a gesture of remorse coupled with spite you put the liquor bottles in the woodbox, where momentarily you hope that nobody will find them until the first cold day.

It is among certain types of prosperous urban intellectuals that one is likely to find the ultimate in pretentious potluckism. Their casseroles contain the most eccentric mixtures, their Bohemianism is the most slavishly studied. They are given to having informal hideaways not far from the city in a wood that harbors a mosquito bog. There they go to get away from the sophistication of urban life . . . their own private little Hooverville.

The more nearly the doors fall off their hinges, the bigger the holes in the knees of their blue jeans, the happier they are. They are "living life," and the Cadillac is drawn up by the shack ready to take them back to Town, scrubbed and polished the first thing Monday morning.

In general it is only the well-to-do who carry the cult of informality this far, because only to them does total informality mean a change in pace and therefore a party.

It may seem strange to the reader that hosts and hostesses should be separated by so vast a chasm from guests. Aren't they the same people? Curiously they are not. Rarely does a host behave toward his own guests as he would want a host to behave toward him. Put in a position of responsibility and authority a change comes over him. The very same man who dislikes to have a fuss made over him when he goes visiting, will make a considerable to-do over the friends who come to visit him. The ones who do not like to have their time planned for them are the very ones who worry most about not having made arrangements to entertain their guests. The ones who help themselves most liberally when they are guests are appalled at the gluttony of their friends when they are hosts.

Unquestionably the perfect host is the one who makes a compromise between what he wants and what he thinks his guests want. If he does that he may hit somewhere near the truth. But even this can lead to confusion as compromise sometimes does. My father, who like most clergymen hoarded anecdotes at the expense of his own profession, used to demonstrate what compromise meant with a story about the dean of a divinity school who was entertaining a distinguished company of bishops and professors of theology at luncheon in his house. He had just bowed his head to say grace when the maid appeared from the pantry and announced, "Bishop Smith on the phone for you, Dean Barkley." This raised a fine theological point in the dean's mind. Should he answer the telephone and keep the Lord waiting for grace, or should he say grace and keep the bishop waiting? A moment later he bowed his head over his plate, "Dean Barkley speaking," he said.

Such confusion between the dictates of hospitality and the dictates of conscience are not uncommon. The dean was being at the same time the guest of the Lord and the host of the bishops. For most of us hospitality is not a theological question and therefore should be a simpler matter, but we are torn in much the same way—between our desire to be good hosts and our impulse to maintain our privacy.

The perfect balance for which we strive in the relationship between guests and hosts is of such delicacy that only rarely can it be achieved. It is because we do sometimes achieve it that we are continually trying to find it again. It is as likely to happen by accident as by intent and nearly as often with those who are almost strangers as with old friends. The chemistry of true hospitality is compounded of convenience, comfort, congeniality, and conversation; or, if you prefer to eliminate conversation, then you agree with Mr. Emerson, who wrote in his Journal about a century ago: "Hospitality is a little fire, a little food, and an immense quiet."